This Book
Belongs To:

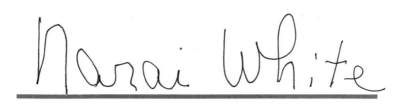

GOLDILOCKS AND THE THREE BEARS
AND OTHER STORIES

from the
Best Loved Stories Collection

Copyright © 2004 by Dalmatian Press, LLC

All rights reserved
Printed in the U.S.A.

Cover Design by Bill Friedenreich

The DALMATIAN PRESS name and logo are trademarks
of Dalmatian Press, LLC, Franklin, Tennessee 37067.
No part of this book may be reproduced or copied in any form
without the written permission of Dalmatian Press.

ISBN: 1-40370-749-9
13145-0604

05 06 07 08 LBM 10 9 8 7 6 5 4 3 2

Best Loved Stories Collection

GOLDILOCKS
AND THE
THREE BEARS
AND OTHER STORIES

DALMATIAN PRESS

Table of Contents

Goldilocks and the Three Bears

Retold by Jackie Andrews

Illustrated by Lawrie Taylor

Once upon a time there were three bears who lived in a cottage deep in the heart of the woods. There was a great big father bear, a middle-sized mother bear, and a teeny weeny baby bear.

Every morning they cooked porridge for their breakfast, and every morning they all went out for a walk in the woods while their porridge cooled.

One day, while the three bears were out enjoying their morning walk, a little girl named Goldilocks was also out in the woods.

She had been picking flowers and had wandered rather a long way from home.

"Oh, dear," she said. "I hope I find a house soon. I think I'm lost. I shall have to ask someone the way home."

And then she saw the cottage where the bears lived.

Goldilocks knocked on the cottage door. There was no reply.

"Oh, there's no one at home," she said, disappointed. Then she turned the handle and found that the door wasn't locked.

"But I'm sure they won't mind if I go in and wait for them."

And that's just what she did.

Goldilocks stepped into the kitchen and looked round. It was all very neat and tidy and there was a wonderful smell of porridge in the air. It made her feel very hungry.

She went over to the table and saw the three bowls of porridge: a great big bowl, a middle-sized bowl and a teeny weeny bowl.

"It won't hurt to have just a little taste," she said. And she pulled out the biggest chair.

It was Father Bear's great big chair.

Goldilocks sat down and tried the porridge in the great big bowl.

"Ow, ow!" she cried, dropping the spoon. "This porridge is far too hot!"

She went to Mother Bear's middle-sized chair and tried the porridge in the middle-sized bowl.

"Ugh!" she said. "This porridge is much too cold!"

There was one bowl left. Goldilocks sat down in Baby Bear's teeny weeny chair and tried the porridge in the teeny weeny bowl.

"Mmmm," she said, licking her lips. "This porridge is just right!"

And she ate it all up.

Goldilocks began to feel sleepy. She went into the next room and saw three comfy chairs.

"I'm sure no one will mind if I have a little rest," she said.

She went over and sat in Father Bear's great big armchair.

"Ow, ow!" she cried. "This chair is much too hard."

She went over and sat in Mother Bear's middle-sized armchair.

"Oh, no!" she sighed, as she sank into the cushions. "This chair is much too soft."

There was one teeny weeny chair left.
"This looks just right," said Goldilocks.
And she sat down in Baby Bear's chair.

But Goldilocks was too heavy for the teeny
weeny chair—and it broke!
"Oh, dear!" sighed Goldilocks.
Then she went upstairs to lie down.

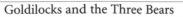

First, she climbed onto the great big bed where Father Bear slept.

"Ow, ow!" she cried. "This bed is much too hard."

Then she tried the middle-sized bed where Mother Bear slept.

"Oh, no," she sighed as she sank into the mattress. "This bed is much too soft."

There was one teeny weeny bed left. "This looks just right," said Goldilocks, and she got into Baby Bear's bed and fell fast asleep.

Now while Goldilocks was sleeping, the three bears came home from their walk. They were looking forward to their breakfast and took their places at the table.

"Look at that!" said Father Bear, in his great big growly voice. "Somebody's been eating my porridge!"

"Oh, my goodness," said Mother Bear in her soft, middle-sized voice. "Somebody's been eating my porridge, too!"

"Oh, no!" squeaked Baby Bear in his teeny weeny voice. "Somebody's been eating my porridge—and it's all gone!"

And it was then that Father Bear noticed their favorite chairs.

"Look at that!" said Father Bear, in his great big growly voice. "Somebody's been sitting in my chair!"

"And look!" said Mother Bear in her soft, middle-sized voice. "Somebody's been sitting in my chair, too!"

"Oh, no!" cried Baby Bear in his teeny weeny voice. "Somebody's been sitting in my chair—and it's all broken!"

The three bears decided to look upstairs in the bedroom.

Up the stairs they climbed. And all this time,
Goldilocks was still fast asleep.

"Look at that!" said Father Bear, in his great
big growly voice. "Somebody's been sleeping in
my bed!"

"My goodness!" said Mother Bear in her soft,
middle-sized voice. "Somebody's been sleeping
in my bed, too!"

"Oh, no!" cried Baby Bear in his teeny weeny voice. "Somebody's been sleeping in my bed— AND SHE'S STILL HERE!"

The three bears all stood round Baby Bear's bed, staring—in amazement—at Goldilocks.

Goldilocks woke up with a start. Unable to believe her eyes, she saw three furry bear faces looking down at her.

"Oh! Oh!" she shrieked.

She tossed back the covers, leaped out of bed, scurried down the stairs, and ran out of the back door as fast as she could. And the three bears were too surprised to say anything.

It was, of course, the last they ever saw of Goldilocks.

The End

The Man,
His Son, and
the Donkey

Retold by Val Biro

Illustrated by Val Biro

A man and his son were going to town. They wanted their donkey to look fit and well so they could sell him for a good price.

Riding him would have made the donkey tired, so they walked behind him, one after the other.

They met some old women standing by
the roadside.

"Look at that," they said. "What a thoughtless
man to let his poor son trudge along the dusty
road when there is a perfectly good donkey
to ride on. Let your poor son ride," said the
old women.

The man thought it would please the old women if he did what they told him. Otherwise they might think he was thoughtless.

So the son rode on the donkey and the man walked in front. The man was well pleased to have taken such good advice.

Soon they met some old men sitting by the roadside.

"Look at that," said the old men. "What a selfish boy! He's riding the donkey while his old father is trudging along the dusty road."

The old men said, "Let your poor father ride."

The son did not want the old men to think him selfish, so he did what they told him.

So the man rode on the donkey and the son walked in front. The son was well pleased to have taken such good advice.

After a while they met some workmen by the roadside. "Look at that," the workmen said, laughing. "What a crazy pair! A donkey is made for two people to ride on, yet the boy is trudging along the dusty road. You should both ride on that donkey," said the workmen.

The man did not want the workmen to think he was crazy. So the man and his son both rode on the donkey.

The donkey was getting tired under the double weight and stumbled from time to time as he trudged along. Some children were playing by the roadside.

"Look at that," they said. "What cruel people! They are both riding on that poor donkey who keeps stumbling along. It should be the other way round! Let the poor donkey ride," said the children.

"How ever could a donkey ride?" wondered the man. But he thought he should please the children, so he decided that somehow he and his son would have to carry the donkey. They got off, and the only way the man could think of was to tie the donkey's legs together over a pole. So the man and his son carried the donkey on a pole.

When they came to the town, everybody laughed at them. "Look at that!" they cried. "Have you ever seen anything like it? They must be quite mad, to carry a donkey on a pole!"

The donkey did not like this and he kicked at the pole. He hated all that noise and was tired of hanging upside down.

The man and his son were just crossing a bridge over a river when the donkey started to kick.

He kicked so hard that the pole broke and the donkey fell into the river.

Splash!

And the man and his son fell into the river, too. *Splash! Splash!* What a calamity—all three splashing helplessly about in the water. And all because the man and his son had tried too hard to please everyone, and in the end had pleased no one!

The End

Henny
Penny

Retold by Jackie Andrews

Illustrated by Lawrie Taylor

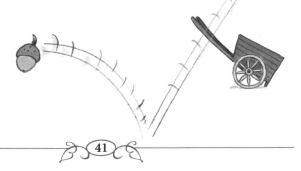

One day, Henny Penny was picking up corn in the farmyard when—***whack!*** An acorn fell and hit her on the head.

"Oh, dear me!" said Henny Penny. "The sky is falling! I must go and tell the king."

Off she went down
the road and on the
way met Cocky Locky,
who said, "Good
morning, Henny
Penny. Where are you
going this fine day?"

"I'm going to tell
the king that the sky
is falling," said Henny
Penny. "A piece of it
fell on my head."

"May I go,
too?" asked Cocky
Locky.

Henny Penny
answered, "Come
along," and they set
off together to find
the king.

They went past trees and past houses and soon they met Ducky Lucky waddling down the dusty road.

"Good morning, Henny Penny and Cocky Locky," said Ducky Lucky. "Where are you going this fine day?"

"We're going to tell the king that the sky is falling," said Henny Penny. "A piece of it fell on my head."

"May I go, too?" Ducky Lucky asked.
"Come along then," said Henny Penny, and
they all set off together to find the king.

They passed a man on a horse and a man with a dog and soon they met Goosey Loosey hurrying along down the dusty road.

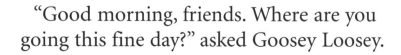

"Good morning, friends. Where are you going this fine day?" asked Goosey Loosey.

"We're going to tell the king that the sky is falling," said Henny Penny. "A piece of it fell on my head."

"May I go with you?" asked Goosey Loosey. "Come along then," said Henny Penny, and they set off together to find the king.

They went through a gate and behind a church and soon they met Turkey Lurkey coming along down the dusty road.

"Good morning. Where are you going?" asked Turkey Lurkey.

"We're going to tell the king the sky is falling," said Henny Penny. "A piece of it fell on my head."

Turkey Lurkey asked, "May I go, too?"

Henny Penny said, "Come along then," and they all went off together to find the king.

They crossed a bridge and went over hills and soon met Foxy Woxy coming down the road.

"Good morning," said Foxy Woxy. "Where are you all going this fine day?"

Henny Penny answered, "We're on our way to tell the king that the sky is falling. A piece of it fell on my head."

"May I go, too?" asked Foxy Woxy.

Henny Penny said, "Come along then," and they all set off together to find the king.

Suddenly, Foxy Woxy stopped in the middle of the road and said, "Oh, dear me, this isn't the best way to the castle. I know a much shorter route. Would you like me to show it to you?"

THE CASTLE

Foxy Woxy's DEN

"That would be very kind of you, Foxy Woxy," said Henny Penny, Cocky Locky, Ducky Lucky, Goosey Loosey, and Turkey Lurkey.

They all went along together to tell the king that the sky was falling.

They went past trees and more trees, and finally they came to a dark hole where Foxy Woxy lived, but he did not tell them so.

Foxy Woxy said, "Here is the short cut to the king's castle. We'll soon get there if you follow me. I'll go first and you come after me, one at a time—Turkey Lurkey, Goosey Loosey, Ducky Lucky, Cocky Locky, and then Henny Penny."

Foxy Woxy led the way into his hole, and waited for them to follow.

And they did. Just as he told them. Turkey Lurkey went in first, and had not gone very far before Foxy Woxy gobbled him up.

Goosey Loosey went in next, and she had not gone very far before Foxy Woxy gobbled her up, too.

Ducky Lucky went next. He had not gone very far either before Foxy Woxy gobbled him up as well.

Then Cocky Locky went in. But as soon as he saw Foxy Woxy, he realized what had happened and called out to Henny Penny, "Run, run!"

Henny Penny ran home as fast as she could.

And so Henny Penny never got to tell the king that the sky was falling, after all.

The End

The Boy
Who
Cried Wolf

Retold by Val Biro

Illustrated by Val Biro

A boy lay in a field all day, looking after his sheep. He lay in the hot sun and the sheep grazed around him in peace.

There was nothing much to do until nightfall, when he would take his flock down to the village, except to keep a lookout for any hungry wolves.

He was very bored, so he decided to play a trick on the villagers. If he shouted for help, as they had told him to do if he ever saw a wolf, they would soon come running to help him chase it away.

He jumped up and ran to the
edge of the field, shouting,
"Wolf! Wolf!"

The men in the village
below came running.
The boy thought it was
very funny to see the old
men come racing to
help him, banging their
shields and waving
their hoes and flails, and
shouting to frighten the wolf away.

The men looked everywhere, but there was no wolf. They went home after counting the sheep to make sure none were missing.

They decided they must have frightened the wolf away with all their noise.

The boy laughed. He thought he was very clever to play such a trick on the villagers.

The next day the boy played the same trick.
"Wolf! Help! The wolf is eating my sheep," he
cried as he ran down the hill towards the village.

Again the men came running to help chase the wolf away. They thought he would be very hungry by now, so they ran even faster and made even more noise.

The boy laughed and laughed as he watched
the men rush up, puffing and panting, shouting
and yelling to frighten away the wolf. But there
was no wolf!

When the men saw the boy laughing, they realized he had tricked them. "Be careful, boy," they said to him. "You will cry wolf once too often." But the boy just laughed at them.

One day a real wolf came into the field—a real, live, hungry wolf, who hadn't eaten for days. He saw the sheep grazing nearby and sprang at them. Up jumped the boy.

"Wolf! Wolf!" he cried as he ran away. He had never seen such a big wolf before, and he could do nothing to protect his sheep, except shout for help. He ran as fast as he could to the edge of the field, waving his arms.

But this time the men did not come.

They heard the boy clearly enough, shouting and crying, "Wolf! A real wolf has come!" but the men took no notice and carried on talking to each other.

The boy could not convince them that there was a real wolf this time. They just laughed at him.

"He is only playing a trick on us again," they said to each other. So the boy gave up and went away.

When the boy came back to the field, he found that the wolf had eaten all his sheep. There was not one of them left and the wolf had gone, too.

The boy sat down. He knew that it was all his own fault. He had tricked the men before with his lies and no one goes on believing a liar— even when he is telling the truth!

The End

The Three Billy Goats Gruff

Retold by Jackie Andrews

Illustrated by John Bennett

There were once three billy goats who lived in the mountains, where wild-flowers grew and eagles had their nests. There was Big Billy Goat Gruff, Little Billy Goat Gruff and Baby Billy Goat Gruff.

They roamed the high places each day searching for sweet grass and herbs to eat. One day, they came to a deep river. They looked across and could see a meadow full of long, juicy grass on the far side.

The grass looked wonderful, and the three billy goats were very hungry.

"The water looks very deep," said Big Billy Goat Gruff, "but there is a bridge. We can cross that to get to the other side."

Baby Billy Goat Gruff wanted to cross first. *Trip trap, trip trap,* went his little hooves on the wooden bridge.

Now under this bridge there lived a very nasty troll. Whenever he heard footsteps on the bridge, he shouted, "Keep away, or I'll gobble you up!"

And so no one had tried to cross the river for years.

But now, here was Baby Billy Goat Gruff happily trip-trapping across.

As soon as the troll heard him he bellowed, "Who's that trying to cross my bridge? Keep away, or I'll gobble you up!"

Baby Billy Goat Gruff was very frightened. But he said to the troll, in a very small voice, "Please let me cross the bridge. My brother, Little Billy Goat Gruff, is coming next. He's much fatter than me."

The greedy troll thought about this. Baby
Billy Goat Gruff did look rather small. The troll
let Baby Billy Goat Gruff cross over into the
meadow, and he settled under the bridge again
to wait for Little Billy Goat Gruff.

The people who lived nearby were amazed to see Baby Billy Goat Gruff in the meadow.

No one had dared to cross the bridge since the troll came to live beneath it. All the children were taught not to try to cross the bridge—not even to fly their kites in the meadow.

"Be careful of the troll," the children were taught.

"Don't cross the bridge—not even to gather flowers in the meadow."

So the villagers were surprised to see Baby Billy Goat Gruff in the meadow, but they were even more surprised when Little Billy Goat Gruff came along and began to cross the bridge.

Trip trap, trip trap, went Little Billy Goat Gruff's hooves on the wooden bridge.

"Who's that trying to cross my bridge?" shouted the nasty troll. "Keep away, or I'll gobble you up!"

He looked so terrible that Little Billy Goat Gruff almost turned and ran back. Instead, he stood bravely on the bridge and spoke softly to the troll.

"Please don't gobble me up. Big Billy Goat Gruff will be along soon. There is much more of him to eat."

The greedy troll thought about this. "All right," he said. "I'll wait."

And he allowed Little Billy Goat Gruff to cross into the meadow.

The troll settled under the bridge again to wait for Big Billy Goat Gruff.

Big Billy Goat Gruff was now very hungry.
He had climbed back up the hill so the troll
wouldn't see him watching.

He could see the river from the hillside, and as soon as Baby Billy Goat Gruff and Little Billy Goat Gruff were safe in the meadow, he trotted down to the bridge.

Trip trap, trip trap, went his hooves as he ran on to the bridge. The nasty troll heard him.

"Who's that trying to cross my bridge?" he shouted. "Keep away, or I'll gobble you up!"

Big Billy Goat Gruff snorted and stamped and bellowed.

"Just try it!" he said, and he lowered his head and—*whump!*—butted the nasty troll right off the bridge.

The troll fell down, down into the river. He disappeared into the water with a great *splash!* and was never seen again.

Baby Billy Goat Gruff and Little Billy Goat
Gruff ran to meet Big Billy Goat Gruff as he
trotted over the bridge into the meadow.
"We knew you would beat the troll," they said.

All the people came out of their houses and
ran into the meadow. They could cross the
bridge as often as they liked now: there was no
nasty troll to stop them.

They brought honey cakes, carrots and little cream cheeses for the three billy goats to eat, and the children put flower chains round their necks.

The three Billy Goats Gruff spent the rest of their days in the beautiful meadow and everyone was happy.

The End

The Fox
and
the Stork

Retold by Val Biro

Illustrated by Val Biro

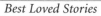

Fox and Stork were good friends and they often spent their days together. There was only one problem—Fox was always playing tricks on Stork.

One day Fox asked Stork to dinner. He wanted to play a trick on her. "This will be one of my best," he thought.

When Stork arrived, he politely showed her into the house. The steaming hot soup was already served, and it smelled delicious. But Fox had played a trick! He put the soup in two bowls but did not lay out any spoons, and he knew Stork would be too polite to ask for one.

Fox began to eat straightaway, lapping up the soup with his long tongue. He cleaned his bowl in no time. But Stork could not drink the soup because of her long beak. How Fox laughed! Poor Stork went home hungry, while Fox lapped up her soup as well.

Now Stork was angry. The time had come for sly Fox to be taught a lesson. She sat down to work out a plan.

"Aha!" she finally said with glee, "I know how to pay him back!" and she went about making her preparations.

Soon after, she asked Fox if he would come to dinner.

Fox arrived at the arranged time. There was the most delicious smell of fish stew in the air and he could hardly wait. Stork put the stew in two jugs with long necks. When Fox sat down, he stared at the table in dismay. There in front of him was Stork's trick.

Clever Stork! She knew perfectly well that Fox would never get his big nose down the neck of the narrow jug, and he would be too polite to pick it up and tip the stew into his mouth.

Now it was Fox who could not eat!

Fox just sat there, glaring at Stork as she delicately picked out the food with her long beak. Soon she had finished her own meal, and she then pulled her guest's jug towards her and ate his as well. So Stork finished both dinners, and Fox went home hungry.

And since then, Fox has always thought twice before playing tricks on Stork.

The End

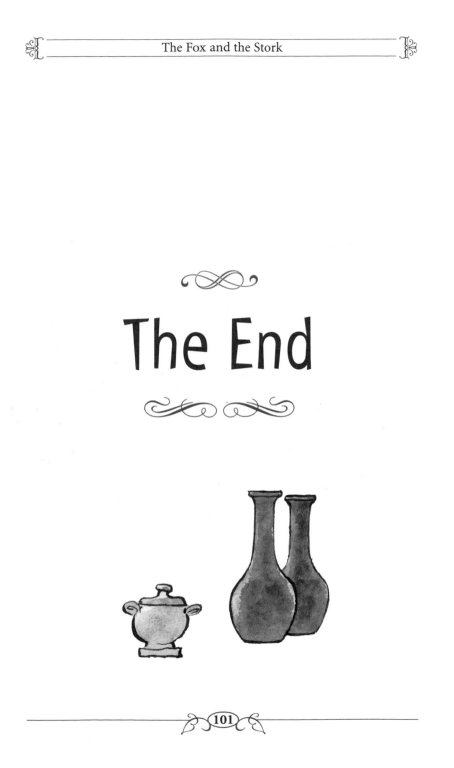

The Hare
and
the Tortoise

Retold by Val Biro

Illustrated by Val Biro

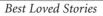

Once there was a hare who could run very fast and a tortoise who could only go very slowly— plod, plod, plod.

One day they met in a meadow.

"I can run much faster than you," said the hare to the tortoise.

"Maybe you can," said the tortoise. He was tired of being teased about being slow, but he knew it was time to teach the boastful hare a lesson. "Let's have a race and see," he said.

"How could a plodding tortoise win a race against me?" said the hare, laughing.

All the animals came to watch the race. They put up a starting line and a finishing post and told the hare and the tortoise to stand side by side on the starting line.

The fox called out, "Ready, steady, go!"

The hare ran fast—hop, hop, hop—for he was the fastest animal in the forest. He ran so fast that he was soon out of sight.

The tortoise crawled slowly—plod, plod, plod— for he was the slowest animal in the forest.

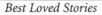

The hare was so far ahead that when he
looked round he could not see the tortoise at all.

"He will never catch up with me," he thought.

It was a hot day and the hare came to a big,
shady tree. "I have lots of time," said the hare. He
stopped for a rest and lay down to sleep—snore,
snore, snore.

Meanwhile the tortoise plodded on steadily. When he came to the big, shady tree he saw the hare fast asleep.

"I must keep going," said the tortoise, and on he crawled—plod, plod, plod. He didn't stop or look round and soon he saw the finishing post ahead.

At last the hare woke up, but it was too late. He jumped up and ran as fast as he could to the finishing post. When he got there he saw the tortoise already crawling past the post with a big smile on his face.

The tortoise had won the race. All the animals were cheering.

"I hope you've learned a lesson," said the tortoise to the hare. "Slow and steady wins the race."

The End